Secret in the Pirate's Cave

THE BOBBSEY TWINS®

SECRET IN THE PIRATE'S CAVE

Laura Lee Hope

Illustrated by Ruth Sanderson

WANDERER BOOKS

Published by
Simon & Schuster, Inc., New York

Library of Congress Cataloging in Publication Data

Hope, Laura Lee.
The Bobbsey twins, secret in the pirate's cave.

SUMMARY: While vacationing in Bermuda, the four
Bobbsey twins become involved with a pair of thieves try-
ing to steal valuable artifacts from the local museum.
[1. Mystery and detective stories.   2. Bermuda
Islands—Fiction] I. Sanderson, Ruth.   II. Title.
III. Secret in the pirate's cave.
PZ7.H772Bogt   [Fic]   80-15070

ISBN 0-671-41118-7
ISBN 0-671-41113-6 (pbk.)

CONTENTS

· 1 ·

Who's Sam?

"I won!" Mrs. Bobbsey cried happily into the phone. "Yes, I won the policemen's charity raffle." She smiled. "It's a trip for two to Bermuda. Isn't that wonderful, Richard?"

Overhearing his mother's news, Bert raced downstairs from his room. "Fan-tas-tic!" he whooped. "When do you and Dad leave?"

Missing the question, Mrs. Bobbsey frowned. "Oh, dear. Are you sure you can't go?" she murmured into the phone. Again there was a long silence and her eyes brightened a bit as she put down the receiver.

"What's up?" Bert asked immediately.

"We're all going away next week!"

"All?" Bert repeated.

"You, Nan, Freddie, Flossie, and me. Unfortunately, your father has too much to do but he thinks the rest of us should go. One thing bothers me, though—Slippery Sam."

"Who's he?" twelve-year-old Bert inquired.

"That's what I asked Lieutenant Jennings who told me I won. All he said was, 'Look out for Slippery Sam when you're in Bermuda!' "

"Maybe he's a crook," Bert guessed.

"Well, I guess it'll be up to my detective family to find out."

Bert went outside where he picked up a basketball and dribbled it under a hoop attached to the back of the garage. He was a good-looking boy, tall, slim—and one of four twins in the Bobbsey family.

The sound of the bouncing ball brought his twin sister, Nan, from one corner of the house, followed by their brother, Freddie, who was six. The girl had a sweet face and snappy brown eyes. She wore her hair behind her ears.

Bert flipped a backhand pass to Nan, and she lobbed it toward the basket. The ball spun around the rim three times before dropping through.

"Pretty fancy," Bert said, as he whipped the ball to Freddie. The younger boy had an impish look in his soft blue eyes. He caught the ball in the palm of his right hand, and with the same motion lofted it toward the backboard. *Ker-plop!* In it went.

"You ll be a Globetrotter yet," said Bert, glancing around for his younger sister. "Anyone seen Flossie? I have some great news."

As he spoke, Freddie's twin skipped into view. In her hands was a box turtle which she tried to balance on the top of her head. Bert shared the exciting news with his brother and sisters.

"Oh, Bert," said Flossie, "can I take Boxy to Bu-mu-da?"

"I'm afraid not," Bert replied. "Mom says no pets on this trip." He added quickly, "We'll be busy looking out for Slippery Sam."

All of the children crowded around their brother, asking who Slippery Sam was.

"Mom doesn't know and Lieutenant Jennings didn't explain."

"Zowie!" Freddie yelled. "Another mystery!"

"We'd better be careful," Nan warned, "in case Slippery Sam is a bad man." Flossie hunched up her shoulders and opened her eyes wide.

That evening, when their father came home for supper, the twins talked only about Bermuda. Richard Bobbsey was a tall, slender man with a strong face and blond hair. He owned and operated a lumberyard in their hometown of Lakeport.

"Tomorrow I expect to have a surprise for

all of you," he told the children.

"Is it about Bermuda?" Freddie asked.

His father nodded and quickly changed the subject. "You know, kite flying is a big sport on that island."

"Really?" Nan said.

"I was there once," Mr. Bobbsey replied. "Many years ago. It was during Easter and on Good Friday the sky was filled with thousands of kites. It's a custom in Bermuda."

After the children cleared the table and put the dishes in the dishwasher, the boys went down to the basement and found an old kite. Bert blew the dust from the red tissue paper and inspected the sticks.

"It'll still fly," he said. "And I guess the tail's long enough." A thick stick, wrapped with string, lay beside the kite.

"If there's wind tomorrow, I'll take it down to the playground and fly it," said Freddie.

Next morning, Freddie jumped out of bed to find the weather cool and breezy. Just what he had hoped for! After breakfast he grabbed the kite and started out the back door.

"May I go with you?" Flossie asked.

"Sure, come on!"

They ran out of the yard and down the street with the kite wobbling two feet above Freddie's left shoulder. The schoolyard was several blocks away. It was an ideal place for kite flying. When they reached the school, no other children were in sight.

"Here, Floss, you hold the kite, but don't step on the tail," Freddie said. The girl's chubby fingers grabbed the end of the tail stick and she held it above her head while her brother let out fifty feet of string.

"All set?" he called out.

"I'm ready!"

"Let 'er go!" Freddie cried and raced off.

The stiff breeze spanked against the tissue paper and the Bobbseys' kite climbed quickly into the air. The tail, made of tied-together strips of rag, snaked back and forth as the kite darted from side to side.

"I wonder if that tail is long enough," Freddie thought as he released the string hand over hand. Finally the kite steadied and rose.

Flossie ran up to her brother. "May I hold the string for a while?"

"Sure, after I let some more out." The boy dropped the ball of cord and freed it fast between his fingers until he came to the bare stick to which the end was tied.

"Oh, boy! She must be a mile high by now!" he said. "Here, you take it, Flossie!"

The girl took the stick. "It's pulling awfully hard, Freddie," she said.

"Don't let go of it!"

Flossie shook her head and kept her eyes on the red spot in the sky.

After a moment Freddie said, "I'd better take it now."

"Don't worry. I won't let go."

"You'd better give it to me anyhow just in case—" Freddie insisted.

"No." Flossie giggled, pulling the kite hard. The red dot twisted about in the sky. It made a loop-the-loop and a nose dive.

"Stop!" Freddie cried, running after his sister.

But she paid no attention. Instead, she yanked harder on the string. The kite leaped higher, then dived steeply.

"You'll break it!" Freddie shrieked.

Suddenly the string went limp in Flossie's hand. The kite wobbled back and forth as if saying good-bye and sank lower and lower.

"See what you did!" Freddie yelled.

"I didn't mean to—" Flossie said, as she wiped away tears with the back of her hand.

"I hope it doesn't get broken," Freddie said.

They ran up one block and down another, looking for the kite which had disappeared from sight. Hopeful, they asked several people if they had seen it. The answer was no. Finally a postman said, "Yes, I saw a kite. It's on the next block—in a tree."

"Thanks." Flossie smiled.

She and Freddie darted around the corner and looked up. There was the kite, caught in the top of the highest tree. Even worse, the branches had punctured the red tissue paper!

"It's ruined," Freddie wailed.

Nanny's Scare

Freddie hurried to the foot of the tree and found the string. He broke it off and wound the trailing piece around his fingers.

As the twins gazed at their ruined kite, Nan appeared on her bicycle. "I've been looking for you," she said. "What happened?"

When she heard what Flossie had done to the kite, Nan said, "Don't worry about it. I have good news! Dad's surprise came today."

"What is it?" Flossie begged.

"It's a telegram from Dr. Malcolm Channing."

"Who?" asked Freddie, wrinkling his nose.

"He's a friend of Dad's," Nan said. "They went to college together." She explained that Dr. Channing was a physician in Bermuda. "And the Channings have two children we can play with, Ted and Pamela."

"Hey, that sounds great!" Freddie said.

The three took one last look at their ruined kite and started for home. When their mother learned about the mishap, she said, "Well, you'll learn plenty of kite tricks in Bermuda."

By bedtime, all the suitcases were packed, and next morning Mr. Bobbsey drove his family to Kennedy Airport in New York. Before saying good-bye, Mr. Bobbsey gave Bert a hug. "Don't forget to take pictures."

"Okay, Dad."

Shortly, the aircraft roared down the runway and lifted lightly into the sky. As it climbed, Bert found an aerial map tucked in the seat pocket in front of him. Bermuda, he learned, was 570 miles east of North Carolina and was a colony of Great Britain. It consisted of numerous little islands which, viewed from the air, were shaped like a fishhook.

"This'll be like going to a foreign country," he told Nan.

"Except that the people who live there speak English," she said.

It seemed no time at all before lunch was served; then, after the trays were removed, the captain announced that Bermuda was below them.

"Would you like something to nibble on?" a flight attendant asked, offering the children a tray of hard candies. As Nan removed the clear cellophane wrapper, she noticed the name "Queen Sweets."

"They're made in London," the flight attendant said. "Tasty. Are your seat belts fastened?"

When all the passengers were snug, the plane glided low. With a small bump, it landed on the runway. As soon as it stopped, Bert unfastened his seat belt and slung his camera over his arm.

The family filed down a portable stairway. Soft breezes and a bright sun greeted them.

"Oh, Bermuda is wonderful," Flossie sighed, taking a deep breath. She and Freddie stayed close to Bert and Nan as they entered the large terminal building. Inside there was a great commotion. Several policemen walked briskly through the crowd as if looking for someone, and a group of boys in bright red jackets was singing and shouting.

Curious, Bert walked up to them. He saw that they wore insignia on their blazer pockets. "What's going on?" he asked.

One of the teenagers replied with a grin, "The captain of our soccer team is leaving for England and we're seeing him off."

Bert smiled. "Mind if I take a picture?"

"Go ahead!"

Bert held the camera to his eye. As he snapped the fourth time, a blond boy with a crew cut dashed out of the crowd directly toward him.

Before Bert could lower the camera from his eye, the boy banged against him and raced away. The camera flew out of Bert's hand and settled next to a woman seated on a sofa. Bert hurried to retrieve it and apologized to her.

"Is your camera all right?" Mrs. Bobbsey asked when Bert rejoined his family.

"The camera doesn't seem to be broken," Bert answered, adding, "That boy sure wanted to get out of the picture."

"He looked as if he'd seen a ghost," Mrs. Bobbsey continued.

"Maybe Slippery Sam was chasing him," Freddie said in a scary voice. Nan and Flossie laughed.

Before anyone had a chance to speculate further, the public-address system boomed, "Will the Bobbsey family please come to the information desk."

Threading their way through the milling crowd, the travelers arrived at their destination. A smiling young woman greeted them. "You must be the Bobbseys!" she said pleasantly. "My name is Kate Bishop."

Nan immediately liked the brown-eyed, chestnut-haired girl, who she guessed was in her early twenties.

"I'm happy to meet you," Mrs. Bobbsey said. "Did Dr. Channing send you to welcome us?"

"Indeed," Miss Bishop replied with a British accent. "I have the family station wagon with enough room to take you all to your hotel."

"Miss Bishop," Bert said, "do you work for Dr. Channing?"

"Yes. I'm the nanny."

Freddie's eyebrows popped up. "You're a kind of goat?"

"No." The young woman chuckled. "I'm a governess. I came from England last month."

"Oh, " Freddie said. "You're a lady governor."

Now everyone burst into laughter. Mrs. Bobbsey explained that a governess was a person who looked after children and lived with their family.

Miss Bishop beckoned Mrs. Bobbsey to the baggage counter where they claimed their suitcases and carried them to the station wagon.

"What a small car!" Freddie said, stretching his arm to reach the roof. He was told that in Bermuda, where roads were narrow, small cars were more practical.

"Most visitors, however, get around on motorbikes or by taxi," Kate Bishop said. When everyone was in the car, she added, "Ted and Pam call me Nanny Kate. I wish you would too."

"Okay, Nanny Kate," Flossie replied cheerfully.

The car rolled from the parking area onto a road which skirted a small bay. "Nanny Kate," Freddie said presently, "do you really know how to drive a car?"

"Yes, why?"

"'Cause you're driving on the wrong side of the street!"

"Oh, don't let that frighten you," the young woman replied. "In Bermuda, just as in England, everyone drives on the left side."

As she sped along, Kate said that American vacationers tended to get confused and often forgot to drive on the left side. She had hardly finished explaining this when a girl on a motorbike suddenly spun toward them. She looked wildly from side to side, her ponytail flying in the wind.

"See what I mean? Driving on the American side." Kate beeped her horn frantically.

"She's panicking," Mrs. Bobbsey exclaimed. Kate slammed on the brakes. The cyclist tried to stop but hit her brakes too hard. The bike skidded and fell on its side, the engine still running. The girl toppled off. Everyone jumped out of the car to help.

"There's a first-aid kit in the glove compartment, Nan," the governess called. Nan grabbed it while Kate and Mrs. Bobbsey rushed to the injured rider.

"Oh, what a stupid thing to do," the girl moaned. She told the Bobbseys she had arrived from New York the evening before. This was her first day of cycling in Bermuda.

"You must be more careful," Kate told her, bathing the scratch with antiseptic.

Mrs. Bobbsey applied the bandage, and the girl rose, shaking from her frightening experience.

Bert, meanwhile, picked up the motorbike, which he and Freddie rolled to the side of the road. As other cars carefully drove past the accident scene, Bert set the bike on its kickstand and got on.

"This is great!" Bert said excitedly. "I bet I could ride one."

"How do you make 'em go?" Freddie inquired.

"I think you turn these things on the handlebars," his brother replied.

He tried this and the back wheel began to spin faster.

"That's right," Freddie said, giving the bike a little push.

"Don't do that, Freddie!" Bert cried, but his warning came too late. He was off the kickstand and traveling at high speed!

· 3 ·

Turtle Trouble

As the motorbike roared on, Bert guided it as best he could. "What'll I do?" the frightened boy thought.

He found the foot brake pedal and pressed gently. It worked. Then he turned left into a meadow of wild yellow nasturtiums. Round and round he went. Finally Bert slowed the throttle and jumped off the slow-moving motorbike. It fell to the grass and stopped.

"That was great!" Freddie cried, running up behind him.

"But you shouldn't have pushed me like that!"

Freddie looked hurt but not for long. He was laughing as the two boys wheeled the motorbike back toward their parked car.

"Phew!" their mother exclaimed. "Don't ever do that again, boys!"

The girl who had had the accident

thanked Mrs. Bobbsey and Kate for helping
her, then limped to her bike and started off.
The Bobbseys climbed back into the station
wagon and once more headed toward the
Deep Sea Hotel located at the opposite end
of the island.

As Bert leaned forward to ask Kate questions, she sighed. "You know, Bert, you re-
mind me of my brother. I wish you could
meet him but—he's run away—all I know is
he's somewhere here in Bermuda."

"How awful!" Mrs. Bobbsey said.

"Is it a mystery?" Nan inquired.

"A very baffling one," Kate said wor-
riedly.

"We're good at solving miseries!" Flossie
volunteered.

"*Mysteries*," her older sister corrected.

"I doubt you could ever solve this one,"
Kate replied, shaking her head sadly.

"We can try!" Nan exclaimed.

The sound of a motorcycle behind them
caused her to turn her head for a second.
Two men were following. Both wore crash
helmets and goggles, and although Kate
pulled far to the left, the motorcycle did not
pass.

"Please tell us about your brother," Nan begged.

Kate said that Tim, who was seventeen, had run away from England. He was a great fan of pirate stories. In a London bookstore he found an old volume telling about West Indies pirates. And in the book he discovered a piece of faded paper with a map of a place called Pirate Island.

"Where's that?" Bert asked.

"From the drawing," Kate replied, "which resembled a fishhook, he could see that Pirate Island was really Bermuda."

"Is that what made your brother run away from home?" Nan questioned.

Kate nodded. "The map showed a cave near Turtle's Head at the end of the island. There was supposed to be pirate's treasure hidden inside."

"I get it," Bert said. "Your brother ran off to find the treasure!"

"I'm afraid so," Kate replied with a sad sigh. "That's one reason I came to Bermuda to work—to look for Tim. Mummy and Daddy are very worried and want him to come home."

Kate explained that Bermuda was full of

caves, hollowed out in the limestone and coral rock. But there was no mention on modern maps of a place called Turtle's Head.

"Can we see one of those caves?" Freddie asked eagerly, as the car rounded a curve flanked by hedges of russet-colored leaves.

"We're coming to one right now," the young woman replied. "Or I should say it used to be a cave. The roof fell in centuries ago, and now it's called Devil's Hole."

"That sounds spooky," Nan said.

"It is, sort of," Kate replied. "It's full of giant turtles, big fish called groupers, and sharks."

"Oh, may we see it?" Flossie piped up.

Kate looked at Mrs. Bobbsey, who nodded in approval. The car was parked and the children got out. Bert noticed that the two men they had seen earlier on a motorcycle also stopped. They went into a store across the street that advertised cold drinks.

"They have no reason to be following us," Bert told himself, then dismissed the thought.

The Bobbseys walked toward a door by the roadside, over which a sign read **Devil's**

Hole. They entered a small curio shop, where they bought tickets, then stepped outdoors again and down a stone path.

At the end of it the children stopped and gasped. Before them was a deep rock hole, the size of their house! And in the clear water, pierced by the sun's rays, swam all kinds of sea creatures!

Kate led the way down a flight of wooden steps until they came to a little bridge built directly over Devil's Hole. From the other end an old man approached.

"How would you like to go fishing?" he asked, wrinkling his face into a smile.

"Sure," Freddie said. "Do we get to keep the fish?"

"If you land them," the man replied.

"Just look at those creatures," said Mrs. Bobbsey as she gazed into the depths. A huge turtle swam slowly beneath them. Then two groupers poked their noses above the surface. They opened and closed their round mouths as if begging for food.

Bert snapped pictures until all his film was used up.

"What's that?" Freddie asked fearfully. He pointed to an underwater nook where a long green snakelike creature waved its body slowly.

"That's a green moray eel," the man replied. "Very dangerous. . . . Well, here are your fishing lines."

From the bridge railing hung half a dozen ropes and on the ends of these the man tied chunks of fish for bait.

"But there aren't any hooks," Freddie protested.

"That's the fun," the man said, winking. "The fish have a chance, too!"

The children let their bait down gingerly. Instantly the fish and the turtles swam to the surface. The water churned as they thrashed about and gobbled the bait.

"I've got one!" Nan shouted. She pulled a fish clear out of the water before it dropped off her line.

Splash! It disappeared into the depths of Devil's Hole.

"I've got a turtle!" Freddie blurted suddenly. The huge creature had the piece of fish in his beaklike jaws, and Freddie pulled hard.

Instantly the turtle jerked its head and the boy who was leaning far over the rail lost his balance.

"Help!" he shouted, his arms and legs flailing in the air. The old man grabbed one leg and Bert the other, while Nan screamed.

"The fishes will eat him!" Flossie cried.

After much hauling, Freddie was returned safely to the bridge.

"It looks as if that turtle was fishing for you," the man said. Afterward, Freddie held the rail tightly with one hand while he dangled his bait with the other.

Before long the hungry fish had pulled all the food from the ropes. "It's time to go," Mrs. Bobbsey finally said.

"If Bermuda's going to be as much fun as this, we'll never want to go home!" Bert

said. Then he turned to Kate. "I've been thinking about your brother again. What does he look like?"

Kate told them that Tim was of medium height and slender, with long, light hair. He was a soccer fan and he liked to play the harmonica.

"Those are some good clues," Bert said, whispering to Nan. "Maybe he's the one who ran into me at the airport!"

"But that boy had a crew cut," Nan said.

After following a winding road several more miles, they saw the sign for the Deep

Sea Hotel. It was a small, villa-type building set on a hill. The entrance was bordered by beautiful green and russet hedges.

"These are called 'Match-Me-If-You-Can,'" said Kate and explained that the bush had no leaves shaped alike.

"How interesting," Nan said. As they pulled up to the doorway of the hotel, a smiling couple stepped out to greet them. The sturdy blond man of about thirty and the black-haired woman said they were Mr. and Mrs. Hutton, the innkeepers.

"And you're the Bobbseys," Mrs. Hutton said. "Welcome to the Deep Sea Hotel."

They were ushered inside. Bert and Freddie had a ground-floor room. Their mother and the girls were shown to a room on the second floor directly above them.

When the baggage had been removed from the station wagon, Kate said good-bye. "I'll call for you after dinner and take you to meet Dr. Channing and his family."

Bert and Freddie immediately unpacked; then Bert took the film from his camera and gave it to the hotel manager.

"Mr. Hutton," he said, "would you please have this film developed for me?"

The manager promised to do it and Bert returned to his room where he set the empty camera on a table near the window.

"I feel hot and sticky," Freddie said. "Let's try the shower, Bert."

The two brothers undressed, tested the water, and crowded into the shower stall together. They laughed and joked and took turns sudsing each other with a slippery bar of soap.

Freddie squeezed the soap through his hands, making it jump into the swirling water on the tile floor.

"That's Slippery Sam," he blubbered, as a sheet of water poured over his face. "Get him, Bert!"

Their high jinks over, the boys stepped out of the shower and toweled themselves briskly. As they dressed again, Bert looked to the table where he had left his camera.

"My camera's gone, and the window screen is open!" he exclaimed.

· 4 ·

Cave Strangers

Bert dashed from their room, down a hallway, and out the door of the hotel. He ran back to the place where the intruder had entered.

Nobody was there. The boy searched the nearby bushes and suddenly came upon his camera. It lay open on the ground!

As Bert picked it up, he was joined by Freddie and Nan.

"Freddie said your camera was stolen," Nan remarked while her brother examined it.

"That's right," he answered, "but the prowler didn't want the camera—only the film, but there wasn't any."

"Who would have taken it?" Freddie asked.

Bert and Nan exchanged glances. Each knew what the other was thinking. "Tim Bishop?" suggested Bert. "He might have been in one of the pictures you took at the airport."

"I don't believe it was Tim," Nan said, "if he's anything like his sweet sister Kate."

Bert's mind flashed back to the two men on the cycle. He smiled to himself. "I sure have a wild imagination," he thought.

After supper in the hotel dining room, the Bobbseys waited for Kate. She arrived with the station wagon promptly at seven-thirty. Bert told her about the incident with his camera but decided not to mention his suspicions.

Dr. Channing's home was only five minutes away. It sat halfway up a beautifully shrubbed hillside and had a white roof like all the other houses in Bermuda. Several hundred yards behind the spacious home stood a stone cliff with great rectangular chunks cut out of it.

The car stopped in the driveway. As the Bobbseys got out, a tall, distinguished-looking man with gray hair stepped from the doorway. He had a mellow, tan complexion and hazel eyes. He was followed by a smiling, smartly dressed woman and two children, who Nan guessed were Ted and Pamela. Both had their mother's wavy hair. The boy, however, was small for his eleven years—he was no taller than his ten-year-old sister. He smiled constantly, while Pamela looked shyly at the visitors.

"We're so happy you're here," Dr. Channing said, shaking hands with them all. "I've only seen Dick twice since our college days. To think I had to wait until you won a trip to Bermuda before I got to meet you!"

"We should visit the States more often," Mrs. Channing added, smiling at her husband as she introduced the children.

"Please come in," Dr. Channing invited, leading the way into an attractive living room. The children made friends instantly. Pamela flashed dimpled smiles as Nan told her about their trip.

The grown-ups talked quietly, sitting on a sofa by the bay window which commanded a view of the rolling green colony.

"I suppose you know something about the formation of these islands," Dr. Channing said with a wave of his hand toward the scene outside.

"I read that they were built by volcanoes," Nan said.

"That's right," Mrs. Channing said. "At one time, Bermuda was a mile high."

"Oh!" exclaimed Flossie. "I'm glad it isn't that high now. We might fall off!"

The others giggled and Freddie asked, "Why are all the roofs white?"

"The only water we get on the island is from rain," Ted began, and before he could explain further, Freddie piped up, "If you want a drink, do you have to stand in the rain and hold your face up?"

Dr. Channing chuckled. "Well, you could do that. But we have a better way." He explained that all the roofs on the island were made of sandstone slates. These were covered with mortar and then whitewashed to help keep the water supply pure.

"And when it rains," their host continued, "the water drains off into a large tank under each house."

"Ted," the doctor suggested, "why don't you and Pam show the Bobbseys the quarry?"

The twins were eager to go, but before they left, Freddie asked, "Dr. Channing, have you heard of Slippery Sam?"

The physician and his children looked at one another as Freddie related what a policeman at home had told his mother.

"Oh, yes." Dr. Channing grinned. "I think you'll probably find Slippery Sam hanging around the aquarium."

"Then we'll go there tomorrow and grab him!" Freddie pronounced.

With that he followed the other children out of the house and up the hill to the quarry. White stone stood in huge columns and a large, symmetrical slab had been cut out at the base of each.

"This is so soft it can be sawed," Pamela explained, pointing to a stack of slate ready to be carted off. "There are lots of little caves around," Ted said. "Like that one up there." He climbed from one ledge to another until he reached a shallow opening in the face of the cliff.

As Nan followed, she said, "Look, it's getting awful dark!"

"Just another rainsquall," Pamela remarked. "The sun will come out again before you know it."

By the time they reached the small cave,

huge drops had already begun to splatter on the children. They pressed close to the wall. Suddenly the rain poured down in torrents.

"It's good we found a place to hide," Freddie said.

"If you built a front on this," Bert remarked, "you would have a nice little house."

"We were thinking about that." Ted smiled. "We've already started to break out small windows." He pointed at two tiny holes the size of half-dollars which had been made in the back wall of the cave. Bert put his eye to one of them, then drew back suddenly and whispered, "I saw somebody!"

"Are you sure?" Pamela asked.

Bert raised a finger to his lips for silence, then pressed an ear against the hole. Voices were coming from the other side.

As the drumming of the raindrops eased, Bert could hear the conversation.

"Those Bobbseys!" a man was saying. "They took the film out of the camera already."

"How'd you learn their names?" came a second voice.

"I called the hotel. Said I was a newspaper reporter asking about new guests."

Bert's jaw dropped. The young detectives had been on the island only a few hours and they already had enemies! These men must be the pair who followed the station wagon and stopped at Devil's Hole!

Now Nan and Ted stood on tiptoes and listened at the second hole.

"We can't follow them too much," one man said, "or they'll get suspicious."

"Yes, if they know Dr. Channing, they must be important. We'd better keep out of sight."

"And tell Tim to lie low too."

Then came a shuffling of feet and the voices ceased.

"We're being spied on!" Bert exclaimed.

"And Tim is part of the gang!" Nan said, worried. "What'll we tell Nanny Kate?"

"The truth, of course," Ted declared.

"Maybe they forced Tim to join them," Pamela suggested.

"What's on the other side of the quarry?" Bert asked.

"A little road that follows the shore," Ted

told them. "It has a few shallow caves."

"How do we get to the other side?" Bert asked.

"Follow me." Ted led the way down the face of the cliff and over a low ridge to the other side facing the sea. Nobody was in sight.

"We'd better go tell Father," Pamela said.

Dr. Channing and his wife were in the living room with Mrs. Bobbsey and Kate when the young detectives arrived.

"I bet they are the suspects the police are looking for," Dr. Channing said, snapping his fingers. He explained that the police were on the lookout for two men who had tried to break into the island museum and steal an emerald cross.

"It's such a beautiful and precious relic," his wife said. "It was found by one of our famous divers in an ancient shipwreck off the shoals."

The doctor said that detectives had been searching Kindley Airport that very afternoon.

"So it wasn't just those soccer players making all the commotion," Bert declared.

"But why are criminals spying on you Bobbseys?" the doctor's wife asked nervously.

Bert wondered whether the photos he took at the airport had anything to do with this strange turn of events and mentioned it. Maybe the would-be thieves were in the pictures!

"And what about my poor brother!" Kate said. "Now I'm more worried than ever."

"I hope my film is ready soon," Bert told Nan on the way back to the hotel.

Next morning Mrs. Bobbsey said that she was going shopping with Mrs. Channing. "What would you all like to do?" she asked the twins.

"We want to go to the aquarium!" Freddie exclaimed.

When Kate arrived with Ted and Pamela, she readily agreed to take them there. She said the aquarium was located by the roadside on a small inlet called Flatts. On one side there was a pink stucco hotel; on the other side, a museum.

"Is that where the emerald cross is kept?" Flossie inquired.

"Yes, and we might see it later," Kate suggested as she parked the car near the aquarium.

The children trooped inside and scattered to gaze into the luminous green tanks of seawater that contained all kinds of fish.

Nan's eye was caught by several light yellow fish with black stripes from head to tail. "Aren't they pretty," she thought and walked closer to read the sign on the tank.

Suddenly she let out a sharp cry. "Here's Slippery Sam!"

·5·

Sweet Clues

"Slippery Sam? Where?" The twins raced toward Nan but could see no one. Their sister was choking with laughter.

"It—it's a fish!" She pointed to a sign explaining that the fish got its name because it was very slippery.

"Oh, gee," Freddie said. "There goes our mystery, pop, like a balloon."

Bert grinned and shook his head. "I guess the Lakeport police department knew we'd fall hook, line, and sinker for their joke!"

After they saw all the pretty colored fish, they left the aquarium and started toward the museum next door.

Inside, a lady attendant directed them to a tall, glass-fronted safe. A radar detection box was mounted on top. The safe was lit up, showing rare treasure found on an old wreck on the Bermuda reefs.

Slippery Sam

"Oh, look! There it is!" Nan pointed to a beautiful gold cross about four inches high and studded with large emeralds.

"And see those gold bars too," Bert remarked.

The attendant overheard him and explained, "These treasures are worth well over a hundred thousand dollars. That's why we guard them so carefully."

"Do you think those men may come back and try to steal the cross again?" Nan asked.

"It's possible," the woman said, "but I hope the police will arrest them soon."

"What about clues?" Bert asked.

The attendant shrugged. Bert whispered to Nan, "Let's look around for some. Maybe we can help the police."

While Kate chatted with the attendant, the Bobbseys and their friends began to look around the museum. They glanced under display cases full of shell collections and old island relics.

"What's this?" Flossie asked, picking up a piece of twisted cellophane wrapper. The name on the paper read "Queen Sweets." The same kind the flight attendant had served on the plane!

"Probably dropped by one of the sight-seers here," Bert said.

"We'll keep it anyhow," Nan decided.

The children thanked the woman and walked out the far door of the museum into an open-air zoo. The Bobbseys had seen larger ones at home, but zoos were always fun.

On either side of a long path, colorful birds preened themselves, and in a large cage there was a collection of monkeys. Bert and the girls went to look at the birds while Freddie raced toward the monkeys.

Flossie was interested in a small black bird with a yellow bill. As she approached it, she heard a voice say, "Oh, hello!"

The girl looked around to see who was speaking.

"Is this little bird really talking?" asked Flossie, tugging at Kate's hand. She saw the yellow beak open and shut. "I'm a bird, I'm a bird!" came the reply.

"It *is* talking!" the girl exclaimed.

"Good morning, good morning!" the bird said.

"That's a myna bird," the governess explained. "He's quite a chatterbox, isn't he?"

"Good-bye, good-bye," called the bird as the children turned to a flock of pink flamingos strutting in the sunshine.

"Look!" Bert said. "Their knees bend backward!"

Suddenly they were startled by a wild scream. Freddie! They turned around and ran toward the monkey cage. Freddie put his finger through the bars and a monkey was nipping it!

"Ow, ow!" the boy cried out.

When the shouting children ran up, the monkey let go and Freddie shook his finger.

Nan scolded him. "Don't you know you shouldn't put your finger in a cage?"

"I didn't know the monkey was hungry."

"You shouldn't tease monkeys," Kate said, looking at the boy's finger. It had a red mark, but the skin was not broken. She took Freddie to a fountain and let the cold water run over his finger.

"It's all right now." He grinned. "I'm hungry like that monkey, Nanny Kate. When are we going to have lunch?"

"Right now. I know a good place," she replied, and led the children out of the zoo. They followed her across the street and around the corner into a small restaurant in Flatts. The waitress put two tables together, and Kate said, "How would you like a Canadian burger?"

"What's that?" Bert asked.

They were told that it was a bun cut in three layers and filled with chopped meat, cheese, and lettuce.

"Hm, sounds good," Nan said.

When the sandwiches were served, Bert took a big bite. "Boy, this tastes great!"

Spotting the restaurant owner, Nan asked her, "Do you sell Queen Sweets here?" and showed her the wrapper.

"No, but I've heard of them," the woman said.

As she spoke, an old man came in the door and found a seat in the corner of the restaurant. He watched in amusement as the children chatted away.

"Those thieves had some nerve trying to steal that beautiful emerald cross!" Pamela remarked.

"Yes," Bert said, "especially with that radar warning system."

"I think the crooks were outsiders, and not Bermudians," Nan ventured. "The people here are so nice."

"Maybe they came from England and had a supply of the candy with them," Ted guessed.

Bert reasoned that perhaps the thieves were treasure hunters who thought it would be easier to steal the valuable relics than dive for them.

"Nanny Kate," Bert said, "did the police look for any new treasure hunters on the island?"

"I really don't know."

The old man in the corner pushed back his chair, wiped his beard with a napkin, and said, "Treasure, did I hear you say?"

The children turned their heads. "Yes," Bert said. "Do you know about any?"

The man chuckled. "Did you ever hear of George Washington's treasure?"

"No," Nan said. "What was it?"

"A hundred kegs of gunpowder."

"That's no treasure," Freddie said.

"It was for George Washington," the man continued and told them an old Bermuda tale.

During the American Revolution, the Yankees desperately needed gunpowder, and the Bermudians, loyal to the king, had a supply in Gunpowder Cavern. An American ship was sent to the island, and while it was dark, anchored in Tobacco Bay. A group of men went ashore and carried off one hundred barrels of gunpowder.

"Some people say the Bermudians gave it

to the Americans in exchange for food," the old man concluded, "but nobody knows for sure."

"Is the cave still there?" Bert asked.

Kate nodded. "At St. George," she said.

"Oh, can we go there?" Freddie asked eagerly.

"Yes, I think that would be fun," Kate replied.

As the children started to leave, the old man took a candy from his pocket and unwrapped it. Bert passed close to his table and glanced down at the wrapper. Queen Sweets!

The boy's heart pounded with excitement. Could this be the suspect?

Caught!

Should Bert say something to the old man right now? No—play it cool, he decided.

Motioning to Kate to wait a moment, Bert asked the restaurant owner, "Do you know that old man over there in the corner?"

"Yes, that's Will Simpson."

"Has he been around here long?"

"As long as I can remember. He's a boat repairman. Nice old fellow."

"Thank you." Bert went over to the man who was still sitting at his table. The other children watched intently as Bert asked him about the sweets.

"I'll tell you where I got the candy; it's no secret," Will Simpson said. "A fellow gave it to me for answering some questions."

"What kind of questions?" Bert asked.

The old man peered into the twins' eyes.

"You act like the whole Bermuda police force. I didn't do anything wrong."

"We didn't say you did." Bert smiled. "But we think the fellow who gave you the candy might be wanted by the police."

"They didn't look like criminals," the man said in alarm.

"They?"

"Yes, there were two of them." After some more prodding, he went on. "They asked me mainly about the museum—when it opened and when it closed."

"That's a great clue," Nan whispered to her brother. "Shouldn't we tell Dr. Channing?"

Bert went immediately to a telephone booth. When he told the doctor what he had learned, Dr. Channing said, "Stay right where you are and don't let Mr. Simpson leave either."

Bert returned to the table and did his best to keep the conversation going so that the boat repairman wouldn't leave. The old man pulled a piece of candy from his pocket and munched on it until a police car pulled up in front. Two young officers stepped out, introduced themselves, and then began to question Mr. Simpson further.

"Could you describe these two men?" one of them asked.

The old fellow said that one man was young, muscular, had jet black hair and a square jaw. The other, about forty, was the man who asked him the questions. He had thin, sandy hair and blue eyes.

"Any identifying marks?" the officer asked.

Mr. Simpson paused, then said, "Yes, he has a diagonal scar over his upper lip."

Writing down Mr. Simpson's address, the policemen thanked him for his information and left.

The boat repairman chuckled. "I've never seen kids helping the police like that before," he said. "You're pretty smart."

"Now we're off to Gunpowder Cavern," said Kate. "Come on."

On the way to the station wagon, Bert whispered to Nan, "I wonder if those two guys were the same ones we heard talking in the cave near Doc Channing's house."

They all piled into the car and Kate turned again at the corner, went past the museum, and headed east along a road which skirted the north shore of the island.

"Oh, how pretty the water is," Flossie said, looking at the great sparkling ribbons of blue and green.

"The town of St. George where we're going," Pamela said, "is the oldest place on the island. It was founded in 1612."

"That's eight years before the pilgrims landed in the *Mayflower!*" Nan said.

Kate mentioned that the big town of Hamilton, near the center of the island, was settled later. She added that a group of English people, called the Virginia Company, decided to live in Bermuda after their ship, the *Sea Venture*, was wrecked off St. George in 1609.

"Ooh—shipwrecks and pirates!" Freddie gleamed. "I wish I lived way back then."

"It wasn't easy," Kate replied and told them how the settlers had no animals or vehicles. "They built crude shacks of palmetto leaves and often went hungry."

The road curved past small white houses set among the hibiscus bushes, and neatly dressed children waved as the Bobbseys went by. The girls wore bows on their braided pigtails.

Suddenly the twins recognized the road leading to the airport. Beyond the airstrip Kate turned onto a bridge and minutes later entered a small, old town.

"This is St. George," she said, driving directly to King's Square on the waterfront. The open plaza was flanked on two sides by the town hall and the waterfront where an ancient cannon pointed seaward. Stores and a restaurant stood on the rest of the square. The Bobbseys eyed a raised platform in front of a men's shop.

"What are those funny wooden frames?" Freddie asked.

"Stocks and pillories," Ted explained. "They were used to punish people in olden days."

While the other children ran off to examine the old cannon, Nan climbed up on the platform. She put her head into what appeared to be a large wooden collar.

"I'm glad I don't have to stay in here for hours," she thought in great relief, then tried to wiggle out of the pillory. But she was stuck!

"Help! I can't get out!" she cried.

Several sightseers, snapping photos,

smiled. They thought Nan was only acting.

"Please, will you help me? I'm really in trouble!"

Bert climbed onto the platform trying to stifle a laugh. At the same time, a boy lazied past on his bicycle. The seat was low to the frame and handlebars stood out like tall rabbit ears. He laid his bike against a tree and jumped up to help Bert.

Together the boys tugged at the board which imprisoned Nan's head.

"It must be warped," Bert said, giving it a hard shove. This time the board came loose and Nan pulled her head out.

"Thank you both," she said. The strange boy, who had brown, wavy hair and freckles, looked a little bashful. He seemed to be about Bert's age.

"Glad to help," he mumbled.

Bert extended his hand and introduced himself and his sister.

"My name is Charlie," the boy replied. "I live here."

"That's a nice bike you've got," Bert said as they hopped down onto the pavement again.

"You want to ride it?"

"Sure, thanks." Bert got on the bicycle with his hands reaching up high on the bars. Nan laughed as he pedaled around the square.

Then he stopped and told Charlie, "We're going to visit Gunpowder Cavern."

"It's not far from here," Charlie said. "I'd like to show it to you."

Kate and the girls did not want to leave immediately. "There are shops with pretty clothes to see," she said. "Why don't you boys run along. We'll meet you at the cavern."

"And if we're not there," Charlie said, grinning, "you'll find us at Tobacco Bay."

While Charlie rode slowly along, Bert, Freddie, and Ted walked beside him up a very long hill, past an unfinished cathedral. Its tower stood out against the blue sky. Soon they found themselves in front of a huge gray slab of rock. In it was a doorway, over which there was a sign that read **The Gunpowder Cavern**.

Leaving his bike, Charlie joined the three boys as they mounted a short flight of steps and walked into the gloomy cave. As they explored the dank corridors, Bert said, "Is this where the Yankees came to get the gun-powder?"

Charlie nodded. "Come on. I'll show you where the boat was hidden that carried the barrels to General Washington."

Outside in the sun again, the boys blinked, then followed Charlie down a hill past a small shack to the edge of the bay.

"This is where the little boats came in from the ship," Ted explained.

With the breeze blowing in from the sea, Bert gazed out over the water. He could imagine what it had looked like in olden times—the American ship standing offshore in the darkness and the men quietly rowing in to seize the ammunition.

As they watched, Ted and Freddie scrambled down the bank to the water's edge and skirted the marshy shore of Tobacco Bay.

They were nearly out of sight when cries came from Freddie. "Hey, look what we found!"

Bert and Charlie hurried after the other boys and discovered them digging with sticks up on the beach.

"It's an old boat we discovered," Freddie

said excitedly. "Maybe it was left here by pirates!" Sand nearly covered the rowboat.

"If we dig it out, can we keep it?" Ted asked.

"I don't know," Bert replied. "It doesn't belong to us."

They turned to Charlie, who said that he had never seen the boat before. "But I don't come down this way often," he added.

Just then Kate and the girls appeared on the bank high above them. "What did you find?" the governess called.

"A pirate boat!" Freddie cried. "Come on down!"

Kate decided to stay with the car but the girls joined the boys.

"Let's play pirates," Flossie suggested.

She took her twin brother's hand and jumped up and down in the old boat while the others talked about dragging it up for repairs.

Suddenly a white-haired man with a black mustache raced down the hill toward them, waving his arms wildly.

"Get out of that boat!" he stormed. "It belongs to me!"

"We—we didn't know," Freddie stammered.

"Who are you?" Charlie asked. "I've never seen you before."

"Never mind who I am," the man snarled. "Scram or I'll call the police!"

·7·

Flossie Flies

The disappointed children stepped back slowly as the scowling man darted past them toward the boat.

At the car they told Kate what had happened.

"Well, it may be his boat," she said. "Anyway, what would you do with it?"

"I could have fixed it," Charlie declared. He shrugged and mounted his bicycle. "I'm going to tell my father about it," he said. "We can come back later and see what's going on there. Good-bye." He rode off, waving.

"What do we do now?" Freddie asked brightly.

"Our secret!" Flossie said. "Come on."

The governess drove the station wagon almost to the square, then turned into a narrow alley and stopped. "Hurry now," she told the girls. "I can't park long. There's not enough room for another car to pass ours."

Nan and Flossie pushed their brothers along ahead of them. Ted and Pamela grinned and remained behind. When they reached the corner, Bert and Freddie stood in the middle of the lane, looking bewildered.

"What—what's this all about?" Bert asked.

"Look at the sign," Nan said, pointing.

On a brick wall was a small sign which read OLD MAID'S LANE. "Ha-ha," Flossie chirped. "You're an old maid, Bert, and so are you, Freddie!"

The Channing children laughed and explained that there were lots of quaint little streets in St. George with odd names. Kate took them around to see BARBER'S ALLEY and FEATHERBED LANE.

"Look at this one," Pamela said, pointing. It read SHINBONE ALLEY.

All along, Bert and Nan kept looking for the two strangers who had followed them on the motorbike. They were nowhere in sight, yet Bert sensed that the spies were not far away.

It was now late afternoon, and Kate suggested they return to the hotel.

"Thanks for taking us around," Nan said.

"Will we see you tomorrow?" Bert asked.

"Of course," Ted said. "We have to solve these mysteries before you finish your vacation!"

It was agreed that their friends would come by after breakfast the next morning.

When they left, Bert raced into the hotel and went directly to Mr. Hutton. "Did the pictures come back yet?"

"I'm afraid not," the innkeeper replied. "You'll have to be patient, Bert."

After supper that evening the two older children played Ping-Pong in the hotel game room. Their mother and the younger twins watched until Flossie fell asleep on the sofa. Mrs. Bobbsey lifted her gently and took her to bed. The others soon followed.

They woke the next morning eager for another day's excitement. The sun was shining brightly, and it was quite windy. At the breakfast table Bert said, "I think we'd better eat plenty this morning. Something tells me we're going to do a lot today."

Their waitress, a plump, smiling woman

whose name was Annie, overheard him and winked. She brought halves of grapefruit which she said were from the hotel garden.

"Poached eggs, ham, sausages, and fried bananas are on the way," she announced cheerfully.

Freddie beamed. "I can't wait!" he replied.

When Annie returned with a large tray of food, the boy filled his plate. Upon finishing, he sighed happily. "I'm stuffed. But I'm ready for those crooks!"

As they hurried past the reception desk toward the front door, Mr. Hutton stopped them. "I have a letter for you," he said to Mrs. Bobbsey, handing her an envelope.

"How strange," she murmured, glancing at the Bermudian stamp. "This letter was postmarked at Hamilton."

She opened it and pulled out a piece of folded paper. She frowned deeply. "Oh, this is awful!"

"Mother, what is it?" Nan asked.

Mrs. Bobbsey read, "YANKEES GO HOME. BOBBSEYS NOT WANTED IN BERMUDA."

Mr. Hutton looked shocked. "Who would

ever write such a thing?" He shook his head in disbelief.

"I think we have enemies here," Bert declared, "because we've run into a mystery."

"Someone doesn't want you to solve it?" the man asked.

"It looks that way," Mrs. Bobbsey replied.

"But we're staying, aren't we, Mother?" Nan said. "Nobody can frighten us away!"

"We'd better tell the police about this," the innkeeper suggested, going to the telephone.

A squad car arrived just as Kate drove up in the station wagon with Ted and Pamela. They were amazed to hear about the letter. The police officer took it. "We'll try to trace it for you," he said, "but it will be very difficult."

After the police left, the Bobbseys were driven to the Channing home where they related the incident. The doctor, who had already left for his office in Hamilton, was telephoned. He advised the children to stay close to home while the police tried to track down clues.

When Ted heard this, he said, "Why don't

we fly kites? The wind's good today."

"Let's make them ourselves," Pamela suggested.

The children decided to build a three-stick kite and, at Pamela's suggestion, a round one too. "It's not really round," she said. "It has eight sides, but when it's high in the sky it looks round."

"You mean octagonal," Nan said.

In the basement of the Channing house the children found an ample supply of kite sticks, paper, and string. The nimble fingers of the young Channings worked quickly assembling the sticks. Then Pamela reached into a little cabinet for colorful tissue papers.

The girls selected purple and yellow for their kite, but Ted decided to use all the colors. While he and Bert carefully cut the pieces, Freddie stepped backward onto the kite sticks.

Crack!

"Look what you did!" Flossie exclaimed.

"I—didn't mean to," Freddie quavered.

"Don't worry about it," Ted assured him. "We've got lots of sticks. Look at these." He showed some long slender ones standing in the corner of the basement.

Freddie's eyes widened. "Why don't we make a giant kite?"

"Okay," Ted agreed. "Of course we'll have to use double-thick brown paper."

When the boys' kite was complete, it stood two feet taller than Bert.

"Ours isn't so big," Nan said, standing back to inspect her team's creation, "but I think it's prettier."

" 'Specially with such a nice long tail," Flossie declared.

The boys carried the big kite outside through a basement door that opened onto a patio behind the Channing home. The stiff wind caught it up immediately, and without running, Ted eased the giant higher and higher in the sky.

The round kite took off easily, its tail swishing in the breeze like that of an angry dragon.

When enough twine had been let out, the children took turns holding the strings. Freddie used both hands on the spirited giant kite as it strained in the cloudless sky.

"He wants to get away!" he cried. "But I've got him!"

The girls were content to jiggle the string

of the round kite, watching it dance and dip.

"It looks like a ballet dancer," Nan said.

Holding her hands behind her back, Flossie approached her brother. Rocking back and forth, she asked, "May I hold the big giant too?"

"I guess so, but don't let go!"

Freddie gave the ball of twine to his twin sister. "Got it?"

Flossie nodded. Her chubby fists held on tightly as the big kite tugged.

Suddenly a huge gust of wind swept over the island. The round kite dipped crazily and the other one soared higher. Before anyone could move, Flossie was lifted off the ground!

"Help! Help!" she called out.

Bert and Ted were after her in a flash. "Let go!" Ted shouted, but Flossie clung tightly to the string.

As she started to rise higher, Bert jumped up and grabbed her legs. Together the two of them tumbled to the ground and Ted darted over to grab the string. The little girl laughed and cried at the same time. "That—that's an airplane kite!" she exclaimed.

"Why didn't you let go, Floss?" Nan asked, running up breathlessly.

"'Cause you all—all told me not to," the little girl said.

Having heard the screams, the mothers and Kate raced from the house. They could hardly believe the story. "It's happened before," Mrs. Channing said. "One little child was pulled off a cliff a few years ago. Fortunately, she landed in some straw and wasn't hurt."

"If you hadn't caught Flossie," Kate said, "she might have flown all the way back to New York!"

Even though the governess tried to joke about it, Flossie was still shaking. Ted and Pamela expertly reeled in their kites which prompted Mrs. Channing to ask, "Who wants to go shopping and who'd like to go to the hotel for a swim?"

The boys liked the idea of swimming. After changing into trunks, they hiked to the hotel. They headed for the pool located in the center of a sunken garden behind the main house.

Meanwhile, the three girls, their mothers, and Kate wandered through the shops in Hamilton.

"Oh, look at those wonderful kilts," Mrs. Bobbsey said. She had her daughters try on the short plaid skirts which wrapped around and were fastened by a large, gold-colored safety pin.

"Would you each like one?" their mother inquired.

"Oh, yes!" they chorused.

"Then," Mrs. Channing said, "let me add a little gift too." She walked to a counter which displayed a collection of Scottish brooches.

"These will bring you good luck," she explained as she bought them.

"I wonder what our good luck will be?" Nan said.

"I know!" Flossie grinned at Kate. "We're going to find Tim!"

The shopping over, everyone returned to the car and they drove to the hotel.

As Kate pulled into the long driveway, a man with bushy white hair and a black mustache zipped past them on a motorcycle. The innkeeper, followed by Bert, Freddie, and Ted, chased after him. But the man reached the main road, turned right, and roared away.

· 8 ·

Square Search

"What's going on here?" Mrs. Bobbsey asked.

"That man!" Bert panted. "He tried to get our pictures!"

"He's—he's the same one who chased us away from the boat," Freddie exclaimed.

Mr. Hutton said that the fellow had come to the desk to pick up the photos for the Bobbsey boy. They had arrived only minutes before.

"But I knew the children were swimming in the pool," the manager went on, "and I called to them. When the boys saw the man, they started to chase him."

"And that's when you came in," Bert added.

But who could the white-haired man be? Bert thought he might be the third man in the gang of thieves. But Nan said that did not explain why he ordered the boys to leave Tobacco Bay.

"And why does he want the photos so badly?" Mrs. Channing asked. "Was he in the crowd at the airport?"

Neither the Bobbseys nor Kate remembered seeing him there.

"Have you looked at the photos, Bert?" Pamela asked.

"No, here they are." He pulled out the prints and went through them until he came to the shots taken at the airport.

"Here's the fellow who almost knocked me over," Bert said.

Kate gasped. "That boy there with the crew cut—that's Tim!" she cried out.

"But I thought Tim had long hair," Nan said.

"He's cut it off!"

"And look at that man standing behind him," Mrs. Bobbsey said.

The fellow had sandy hair and a scar was clearly visible on his upper lip.

"That's one of the crooks," Freddie declared. "We have the evidence!"

While Mr. Hutton ran to phone the

police, the Bobbseys and their friends pondered over the latest clue. Obviously, Tim was connected in some way with the suspects.

"I know why Tim bumped into me," Bert said. "He probably saw you, Nanny Kate, and tried to get out of the building as quickly as possible."

"I don't think he meant to damage your camera," Kate said.

Mr. Hutton returned. The police said they would pick up the photo and concentrate their search on the eastern end of the island.

Bert snapped his fingers. "Maybe we can make enlargements of this picture and post them around St. George."

"I have an enlarger," Mr. Hutton said. He volunteered to blow up the negative that evening. When he showed the enlarged prints to the Bobbseys, they were delighted. The details stood out clearly. Nan remarked that Tim's boyish face had a very sad look.

"I agree with you," Mrs. Bobbsey said. "Tim must be torn between hunting for his treasure and returning to his parents."

"Perhaps we can help him do both," Nan said.

Mrs. Channing arrived next morning with Kate and the two children. "How would you all like to go swimming in the surf? I can promise you a big surprise!"

The younger children clamored to go, but Bert said. "Thank you very much, Mrs. Channing, but I'd like to post these pictures in St. George first." He showed her the photos.

"I'll go with Bert," Nan spoke up.

"Fine. After Kate drops us off at the beach she can go with you. Is that all right?"

The children packed their swimsuits, and Kate drove to a pink sandy beach where the Channings had a cabana. Everyone but Kate, Nan, and Bert scampered out of the car.

"Do be careful," Mrs. Bobbsey said.

"Don't worry, we will," Kate said, and they set off for St. George.

Arriving at King's Square, Kate parked the car and they got out to look for suitable spots for the posters. Finally they put one up on the pillory, another on a fruit stand next to the big cannon, the third in front of town hall, and the last on the restaurant doorway.

Underneath each picture Nan had written:

THIS IS TIM BISHOP. IF ANYONE SEES HIM, PLEASE NOTIFY THE BOBBSEYS AT DEEP SEA HOTEL.

The trio lingered in the square until finally Bert said he was hungry.

"How about the restaurant over there?" Nan suggested.

"Yes, I hear it's a good one," the governess said, and they went inside. They found places on a bench beside a long table. A smiling man, who introduced himself as the manager, said that rockfish was their specialty.

"Is that hard to eat?" Bert asked, smiling.

The man looked puzzled at first, then broke into a big grin. "No, rocks in Bermuda are very tender," he replied.

When the fish was served, deep-fried, the visitors found that the white meat was delicious. After they had finished, the manager smiled. "I see you enjoyed that. Have you tried Bermuda lobster yet?"

Bert and Nan said no, and he suggested that they look at some which he kept in a pool behind the restaurant. By this time most of the customers had left and he accompanied them to the lobster pen.

Nan looked down into the water at the huge spiny creatures. "Ugh!" she exclaimed. "I wouldn't like to step on one of those!"

"Here, use this net if you'd like to examine one close up," the man offered.

Gingerly the girl sunk the long pole into the pen. She trapped a big, greenish-red lobster and tried to pull it up. But the edge of the net stuck on the corner of a coral rock.

Nan tugged, and Bert helped her. All of a sudden the net was free. Up through the water it swished. The lobster was hurled in the air and came down on the back of Nan's neck!

"Eeeek!" the girl screamed and jumped back. The lobster fell to the ground.

"Nobody hurt," the manager said, trying to hide a smile. He picked up the lobster and threw it back into the pen.

The three returned to the restaurant and were surprised to see their new friend, Charlie, talking excitedly to Kate.

"Hello," the boy now said, hurrying up to them. "Say, I know your friend!"

"Who?" Bert asked.

"Tim. But he calls himself Jack."

The four walked outside and stood in the shade of the restaurant porch. As questions and answers flew, the Bobbseys learned that Kate's brother lived in St. George.

"I don't know where," Charlie said, "but I know he loves cave hunting."

"What does he live on?" Kate asked. "He doesn't have any money!"

Charlie told them that Tim had a part-time job with a dairy near Fort St. Catherine at the tip of the island. "And you know what?" he went on. "I'm supposed to go cave hunting with him this afternoon!"

"Great!" Bert exclaimed. "We'll go with you and catch him."

"I don't know about that," Charlie said. "Tim is an awfully good runner. If he sees you, he might get away from all of us."

Kate suggested that she and the Bobbseys stay some distance behind.

Charlie agreed. He told them that he and Tim were trying to find a place once known as Turtle's Head. But since no one had ever heard of it, not even old folks, Tim figured that the landmark had somehow disappeared.

"He thinks it's nearby," Charlie continued, "because of some funny rock formations on the shore." The boy glanced at his wristwatch. "Okay. Time to go."

Charlie led them down the street to the edge of the town, then set off along the hilly shoreline.

"Let me go on ahead," he said after a while. The others waited until he was nearly out of sight, then walked along slowly together, trying to look like casual tourists. But their eyes were never off Charlie. Suddenly another boy emerged from behind a clump of dead cedar trees.

"That's Tim!" Kate whispered.

As the two boys talked, Kate became more and more excited. Suddenly, unable to control herself, she hurried forward. "Tim! Tim!" she cried out.

Bert and Nan saw the startled expression on the runaway's face. He turned and bolted off. Trying to follow him, Charlie tripped and fell flat on his face. He rose from the ground, limping, but by the time the trio caught up with Charlie, Tim Bishop was gone!

·9·

Treasure Hunt

"Tim, where are you? If you're hiding, come out!" Kate demanded. Not a sound could be heard, except the distant blast of a ship's whistle.

"It seems as if the earth swallowed him," Nan said, shielding her eyes from the sun and gazing about.

"I think that's exactly what happened," Charlie spoke up. "Jack must have found a secret entrance to a cave. He was going to tell me something important when you ran up."

"You mean, he might have discovered the Turtle's Head cavern since you last saw him?" Kate asked.

"Maybe. Let's look around."

The four held hands and strung out to form a chain. They walked back and forth to cover every inch of ground in an area of a hundred square yards. They looked behind rocks and tugged on the dead cedars. No clues.

"We must find him!" Kate said. "Maybe he's hurt! And if he did find the cave, suppose he can't get out!"

Bert wandered from the group and walked along a low, rugged cliff of coral rock. There was no beach below, only light green water, pierced here and there by jagged rocks.

"A turtle's head must be the clue," Bert thought. If Tim could find it, so could he! The boy walked more slowly now, gazing down into the water. Suddenly he stopped. What was that shadowy thing below?

"Hey, everybody! Come over here!"

"What did you find?" Charlie called out, dashing over the rough ground.

"I don't know yet."

All three stood beside Bert. "See the outline of that rock?" the boy asked.

Kate Bishop gasped. "The turtle's head!"

"It could have been broken off from this," Bert went on, pointing to a rough coral outcropping beneath his feet.

"Then we are near the cave Tim was looking for!" Nan exclaimed.

"Do you suppose he's found the treasure already?" Charlie asked.

"I wonder what it is," Kate said, biting her lip.

Bert continued to gaze down into the water, which the incoming tide churned against the foot of the cliff. He leaned forward for a closer look. The sea had undercut the craggy coral. If there were a cave, it was not visible from that point.

"I wish we could get a view from the sea," Bert said. "We might discover something really interesting."

"We'll need someone with a boat," Kate remarked, "and I think I know just the person. Come on, let's go back."

Charlie promised to continue his search for Tim and also to be on the lookout for the two suspects. At King's Square he said good-bye, and Kate drove back to the beach where they had left the rest of the family. She parked beside the road on top of a steep dune.

Far below, at the foot of what seemed to be a thousand wooden steps, there were colorful cabanas and swimmers enjoying the blue water.

Kate, Nan, and Bert ran down the steps and onto the beach, spotting a fleet of little black snorkels above the water. Several heads bobbed up. Then, one by one the underwater explorers lifted their masked faces.

Freddie and Flossie! Ted and Pamela! The last one to rise was a husky man in a skintight black diving suit, who carried an oxygen tank on his back.

"What kind of treasure did you find this time, Pam?" he boomed. The girl opened her hand to reveal several tiny shells.

"What, no gold bars?" the man said and splashed to the shore.

Flossie raised her goggles and ran to hug Nan. "Look who we met here." The diver grinned. He had a broad, tanned face and his eyes crinkled at the corners.

Kate made the introductions. "Nan, Bert, this is Walter Murdock, Bermuda's most famous diver. He's the person who just might be able to help us."

The man extended his hand. "Just call me Wally," he said. "Too bad you weren't with us today. We've been treasure hunting!"

"Wally," Bert said, "are you the man who found the gold in the old shipwreck?"

The diver nodded and Bert continued. "Perhaps you can help us. We're looking for a secret cave near St. George."

Before Bert or Nan could tell him any more, Flossie tugged at his hand. "You promised us a ride in your boat."

"Sure, let's go." Wally smiled.

The little girl scooted down the beach to a cove where a motorboat was anchored. Wally flippered along, followed by the other children, while Kate watched from the sand.

As Nan stepped into the boat, she exclaimed in surprise, "Look! It has a glass bottom!"

"That's so you can watch me swim around on the ocean floor," Wally said. "Treasure hunters, are you ready?"

"Yes! Yes!" Flossie exclaimed happily.

Wally started the engine, and the motorboat glided swiftly out into the blue sea.

"Bert, you take charge while I dive," Wally said after a while. Then he stepped over the side and disappeared.

"Look, there he goes," Freddie cried, pointing down through the glass bottom. Far beneath them in the bright, clear water they saw Wally swimming gracefully. He picked up a coral fan and held it over his head for the children to see.

"I want to be a diver too!" Freddie declared. He found a place to sit on the edge of the boat, and Flossie joined him. "Hey, Bert," Freddie said, turning around quickly, "look over—"

Splash!

Freddie had bumped Flossie with his elbow and the little girl dived headfirst into the water.

"Oh, there she is, under the boat!" Nan cried out, as her sister, looking like a water baby, sailed beneath her.

Wally moved like lightning. He zipped up under the boat, grabbed Flossie, and popped to the surface. She coughed and sputtered as Bert and Nan lifted her back into the boat.

"See what I found—a Flossie Fish," said Wally, grinning. The frightened child who was about to cry changed her mind and laughed instead.

"Ha-ha, look at Slippery Flossie!" Freddie teased.

The diver lifted himself back into the boat, started the motor, and guided the craft ashore.

The younger ones jumped out onto the sand and raced to tell their mother what had happened while Bert, Nan, Ted, and his sister lingered behind to talk to Wally.

"Speaking about treasure hunters," Bert began, "have you seen any strangers lately who looked suspicious to you?"

Wally removed his flippers, tossed them into the boat, and looked thoughtful. "Come to think of it—there are a couple of fellows on the island I wouldn't trust."

"Who are they?" Nan asked.

"Harvey and Joe," the diver explained. "They worked with me for a while, then one day left without any warning. Ever since, some of my diving gear has been missing."

"Did you tell the police?" Bert inquired.

"No. Those guys left some shortwave radio equipment in my boathouse. I'm sure they'll be back to claim it, and then I'll ask about the diving gear."

Bert took a deep breath before he posed the next question. "What did these men look like?"

The children were not greatly surprised when Wally Murdock described the two suspects perfectly. They told Wally all they had learned about the men.

"Have you touched the radio receiver?" Bert asked.

"No. Why?"

"Then the police can take fingerprints," Bert pointed out.

Wally thought that would be an excellent idea. If the authorities could identify the men and learn something about their backgrounds, there would be a greater chance of finding the suspects and making an arrest.

Bert and Nan also told Wally about Tim and the lost cave.

"I'll tell you what," Wally said, pointing to his boat. "We'll take a ride around the coast and look at that cliff. Maybe there is an opening near the base."

While Wally changed his clothes in a cabana, Nan and Pamela got permission from their mothers to go with the diver.

"I'll see that the children get home safely," Wally called back, and they all hopped into the boat. The diver pushed it out, started the motor, and off they cruised.

Half an hour later, Bert pointed. "There's the place!"

"Who's that boy waving his arms at us?" Wally asked.

"That must be our friend Charlie," Nan said. He was making frantic motions toward a low spot on the shore several hundred yards away.

Wally pulled in close and Charlie leaped aboard, excited.

"I found something!" he said, after being introduced to Wally. All three listened as the boy poured out his information. He had found the place where Tim was living: a shack near the sea not far from Tobacco Bay. After making inquiries of several neighbors, Charlie learned that two men had moved in with the boy recently.

"Yesterday all three disappeared," he said. "And you know what? That old boat's gone too!"

· 10 ·

Discoveries

"Where is this shack?" Ted asked.

"We passed it on our way to the boat at Tobacco Bay, remember?" Charlie replied.

Nan thought they should examine the place for clues. "Please come with us, Wally."

"Indeed, I will. You may need protection."

Wally Murdock moored his boat, then hurried with the children to King's Square. There he hailed two taxis which sped them to Tobacco Bay.

The cars stopped and they got out. "There's the shack," Charlie said. "It was built by fishermen years ago. It has one big room. We used to play there after it was abandoned."

Bert ran down the path and gingerly

opened the front door. It squeaked on its rusty hinges, letting in sun over the earthen floor. The boy entered, followed by the others.

"Poor Tim," Pamela said, "living in a place like this!" Two wooden crates, side by side and stained from spattered food, served as a table.

In one corner lay a cot, its ripped canvas bottom crudely mended with brown twine. The only other furniture there was a worn-out easy chair. Stuffing protruded from a tear in one arm, and broken springs hung down underneath.

"Let's look everything over carefully," Bert suggested. His toe kicked up some old newspapers and he bent down to examine the dates. They were recent.

Nan peered under the cot, while Ted rummaged through some paper bags. He pulled the dusty cushions from the old sofa and his fingers felt into the crevices.

"Hey, what's this?" he suddenly exclaimed. He held up a dirty envelope, addressed to Harvey Turner, General Delivery, Hamilton, Bermuda. The postmark was London, but the date was blurred. It contained a note, handwritten on lined paper. Ted read it aloud:

YOU SHOULD BE FINISHED BY NOW. AS OF THE TWELFTH WE'LL BE STANDING OFF BERMUDA. FOLLOW OUR PLANS. ROGER.

"The twelfth!" Bert said. "That's today!"

"But it doesn't say what month or year," Wally Murdock remarked. "This note could have been lying around for a long time."

"But if it is today," Nan said, "we'll have to do something fast!"

All agreed that the thieves might run off to a getaway boat off the coast.

While Nan was thinking hard about what to do next, her eyes fell upon a small photo half buried by dust on the earthen floor. She picked it up, brushed it off, and gasped. "Look at this! A picture of Kate and Tim, and that must be their mother and father!"

Suddenly Pamela said, "Hush, everybody! Here comes someone!"

Bert glanced through the window toward the top of the hill, where a boy walked hesitantly toward the shack.

"Get behind the door!" Wally ordered.

They all waited quietly, their nerves tense. Bert peeked out through a crack.

"It's Tim Bishop!" he whispered.

Ten feet from the door the boy stopped and looked back over his shoulder. No one was in sight. He pulled out a flashlight, and with a catlike movement dashed into the shack. As he did, Bert slammed the door shut. With a cry of fright, Tim Bishop whirled about.

"Don't be afraid, Tim," Bert said.

"Your sister Kate is worried sick about you," Nan said. "And your parents too."

The young man looked around. He was wild-eyed. "Are you going to have me arrested?"

"Have you done anything wrong?" Pamela asked.

"No."

"Then why are you worried?" Ted inquired.

"It's those two men," Tim said, looking ashamed. "Turner and Sanderson."

The boy suddenly noticed the photo Nan was holding. He reached forward and took it. "Thanks. That's what I came back for," he said. "I left it when we moved to the—"

"—cave?" Charlie asked. "We know you found one because you disappeared near the Turtle's Head rock."

Tim looked up in surprise. "You—you found it too?"

"Bert Bobbsey did," Charlie replied and introduced Wally Murdock and the rest of the group. "Your sister is the new nanny for Ted and Pamela," he added.

Wally asked, "Does anyone else know about the cave, Tim?"

"Yes! Turner and Sanderson!"

"But how did you meet them?" Nan asked.

"Well, I came over to Bermuda to follow up on clues I had found about an old pirate treasure. When I got here I made trips every day to locate the right cave. One day Turner and Sanderson sneaked up on me and made me tell them what I was doing. I teamed up with them because they said they had certain information—of course it was a lie."

"What do Turner and Sanderson look like?" Pamela asked.

When Tim described the two men,

everyone started talking at once.

"Harvey and Joe!" exclaimed Wally. "The thieves who took my diving gear!"

"The same men who tried to steal the emerald cross," Bert cried.

"And no doubt the ones who spied on us," Nan concluded.

"But what about that white-haired guy with the mustache?" Charlie wondered.

"Oh, him!" Tim smiled. "That's Turner in disguise. He got a wig and mustache after you snapped his photo at the airport, Bert. Thought he'd be recognized otherwise."

"So that's why he wanted to steal our pictures," Nan said.

"But the treasure—did you find that?" Bert asked.

"It's not exactly a treasure—yet," Tim replied. He told them he had discovered a thin piece of sandstone slate on which a map was carved. It showed a point of land, a shoal, and an **X** marking a spot offshore.

"On the bottom of it," Tim explained, "is written 'Pirate Wreck.' "

"Is the stone still in the cave?" Wally asked.

"Yes."

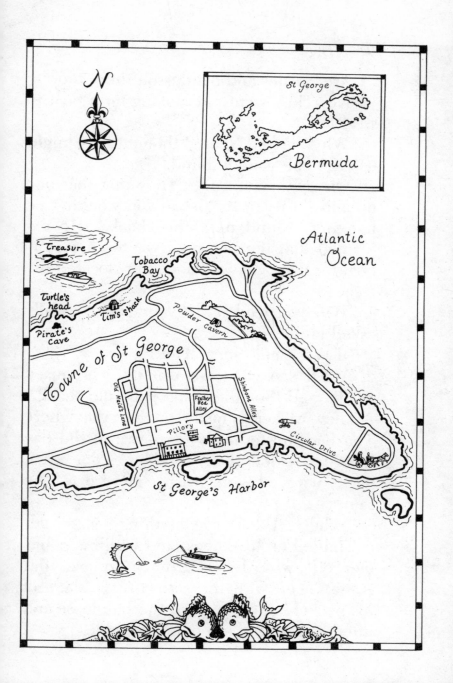

"Are Turner and Sanderson there too?"

"No. They went out looking for a boat to steal."

"Why?" asked Nan. "I thought they might use the one you all found."

"Oh, no," Tim said. "They dug that one up and set it adrift, just so you wouldn't be hanging around near the shack." He explained that the two men wanted a motorboat for their getaway once they located the treasure.

"Will you lead us to your cave?" Wally asked kindly.

"If you'll help me," Tim replied.

"We'll see what we can do," promised Wally, and they filed out of the old shack.

They walked quickly to the spot where Tim had mysteriously disappeared the day before. He led them to a limestone area, partly covered with brush. "Here it is," he said.

"Where? I don't see anything," Nan said.

Tim fell on his knees, and with his palms cleared away debris from a square, flat stone. Then with the screwdriver blade of his pocket knife, he pried the slab loose and lifted it from the top of a deep hole.

"It took me a long time to locate this," Tim said, grinning.

The searchers looked down into the black hole, and Pamela asked, "How do you go down? You don't just drop, do you?"

Tim explained that hand and toe holes had been cut on the inside. "Once you climb down," he said, "there's a giant cave. It's full of stalactites and stalagmites. They look like spears sticking down from the ceiling and up from the floor. It took millions of years of dripping water to form them. Half of this cave is full of water too," Tim went on. "Fifteen to twenty feet deep in some places." He got to his feet and looked around. No one was in sight.

"Look," he said now. "I'll go down and bring that map up." He turned on his flashlight and jammed it inside his belt.

"Let me go with you," Bert volunteered.

"I better help you too," Wally said.

"Wait, Wally," Ted pleaded. "I think you'd better stay here. Just in case those crooks come back."

"All right."

Tim dangled his feet into the black opening, then let himself down, his hands and

feet finding the holes cut into the sandstone. Bert followed carefully.

Topside, the others waited tensely. Nan bent over the hole and called down, "How are you?"

"Okay," came her brother's voice.

"Have you got the stone map?" called Ted.

No reply.

Suddenly another voice—a strange voice—boomed up hollowly from the black hole. "Go away—we've got these kids. So don't try anything funny!"

Nan froze with fright. "Oh! Those two men! They've captured Bert and Tim!"

· 11 ·

Deep Danger

"Let those boys go," Wally Murdock shouted down the hole, "or we'll come down for them!"

"If you try it," the kidnapper called up, "I'd hate to tell you what'll happen to them."

"Oh, please don't go down," Nan pleaded as Ted, Pamela, and Charlie looked on in a state of shock.

"You're right," Wally whispered. "This is a case for the police."

It was decided that Wally and Charlie should stand guard by the cave entrance, while Nan, Pamela, and her brother ran to St. George for help.

The threesome arrived at King's Square out of breath and dashed into the nearby police headquarters. After telling the police what had happened, Nan telephoned the

Deep Sea Hotel. Her mother was waiting there anxiously.

"Mother," Nan said between sobs, "Bert has been kidnapped in a cave and Nanny Kate's brother is with him!"

"What!" The line was silent for a few moments, then Mrs. Bobbsey said in a quavering voice, "We'll all come to St. George right away."

By the time the Bobbseys, Dr. and Mrs. Channing, and Kate arrived, a crowd had gathered around the cave opening, which the police had roped off. It was dusk now, and powerful electric lamps lighted the area. One of the officers was calling down to the kidnappers with a bullhorn.

"Don't harm those boys or you'll regret it! Release them instantly!"

Not a sound came from below.

Upon seeing their parents, Nan and the Channing children pushed through the crowd.

Mrs. Bobbsey tried to hold back her tears while she hugged her daughter. Mrs. Channing held her two children close to her.

Flossie and Freddie walked over as far as they could and tried to peep down the hole.

"Stand back," a policeman ordered. "If those scoundrels are armed, they might shoot up at us!"

Dr. Channing insisted to the police officers, "We've got to do something immediately!"

"You're right, sir. We've waited long enough," their chief replied. He said they had considered lobbing a tear gas shell into the hole. "But that would be harmful to the boys. So we're taking our chances and going down!"

"I'm going with you," said Wally Murdock. He wriggled through the hole. Three policemen followed him, their torches lighting the inky blackness.

When the last policeman had disappeared, Nan darted from her mother's side and skidded feetfirst into the cave entrance.

"Nan! Stop! Come back here!" Mrs. Bobbsey cried out, but the girl's head vanished below the surface and she dropped onto the cave floor beside the startled policemen.

"You shouldn't do this!" Wally told her.

"But I want to find my brother!" Nan replied stubbornly. Then she gazed in amazement around the cavern. The stalagmites and stalactites glowed in the torchlight beams.

"Turner! Sanderson!" Wally cried out. "Give those boys up and you won't be hurt!"

Weird echoes bounced through the cavern but there was no reply from the kidnappers.

"Fan out," one of the policemen ordered.

The searchers pushed ahead, their lights probing every crevice of the glistening cave. Finally they stopped at a deep channel of water.

"Just as Tim said," Wally declared.

Suddenly Nan pointed to a shallow pool between two stalagmites. "What makes those rainbow colors, Wally?"

The man glanced over to where she was pointing. "Oil! That's an oil slick. Somebody's had a boat in here, so there must be an exit out to the sea!"

One of the policemen climbed back up and a call was sent out for a collapsible raft. Minutes later a squad car bounded into sight with a rubber boat. Still folded, the boat was lowered into the hole. Once inside the cavern, the raft was inflated and dropped into the channel. Two policemen got in and paddled in the direction of the sea.

Ten minutes later the sound of dipping paddles returned and the raft appeared under the glare of the floodlights.

"The cave opens to the sea all right," one of the men said. The tide was low, providing enough headroom for a boat to escape.

When the searchers climbed back out, soft weeping could be heard among gruff voices.

Wally Murdock, his chin set with determination, hurried off to his own boat. Suddenly, near the shore, he gave a cry of alarm. "It's been stolen!" He rushed back to tell the others.

"The thieves must have taken it to the cave and carried Bert and Tim off while we were calling the police!" Ted cried.

"With my own boat!" Wally could hardly control his anger. "If I could only get my hands on those devils!"

The next morning all of Bermuda was in an uproar over the bizarre kidnapping. Mrs. Bobbsey had telephoned her husband, who said he would take the next plane out. Meanwhile, the police, assisted by Wally, set out in several boats to inspect all craft in the vicinity.

The diver, using a friend's speedboat, took Nan along with him.

Freddie and the Channing children stayed in Wally's boathouse where the thieves had left part of their radio outfit. Wally had turned it on and commanded, "Sit here and listen. There's only one chance in a million we'll get a signal, but we can't afford to miss it."

Then, while Mrs. Bobbsey went with Flossie, Kate, and the Channings to meet her husband at Kindley Airport, Nan and Wally sped out to a forty-foot cruiser anchored a mile offshore. It bore the name *Green Moray.*

Two men came to the side as Wally's craft approached and the diver told them about the kidnapping. He asked to see their registration, saying that he was authorized by the police to do so.

One of the men, wearing a captain's hat, smiled and handed down his papers.

"Seem to be okay," Wally said, and gave them back.

The man saluted smartly. Then, as the little boat pulled away, he turned to the other fellow and said, "I told you, Roger. Don't worry."

The breeze carried the words to Nan's ears. A chill raced down her spine!

Roger! she thought. Wasn't that the signature on the mysterious London letter?

Out of earshot, she told Wally of her suspicion. "We've got to get back to the police immediately," he decided.

The speedboat churned over the blue waters and pulled up to the dock alongside the diver's boathouse. Freddie raced out, waving wildly.

"What's up?" Wally asked.

"Come here quickly," the boy shrieked. "Whispers are coming out of the radio."

They all hurried inside the boathouse and listened. A hoarse young voice kept saying over and over: *"Green Moray. Green Moray."*

Surprised Pirates

Wally and Nan raced to the radio receiver. The whisper came again. *"Green Moray! Help!"*

"Nan, you were right," the diver said. "Bert and Tim are prisoners on that boat!" He picked up his telephone to call the police. When he hung up, he said, "They're going to send out a couple of launches right now and are picking me up on the way."

"Please, may I come?" Nan begged.

"Mm, this could be pretty dangerous, but—okay. The rest of you ought to wait here, though. I'll call your parents and suggest they come for you."

Not long after he had phoned the message to the Deep Sea Hotel, two police launches appeared in the distance. The Bobbseys cried out in delight when they saw their father!

"Now we can catch those bad men and make them give Bert and Tim back to us," Freddie said.

Mr. Bobbsey told them that Kate had driven everybody to police headquarters. "Mr. Hutton called there and gave them Wally's message. The Channings, Kate, and your mother will be here soon, and they will take you all to a good lookout point to watch the capture," he said.

Nan pleaded to be allowed to go in the boat with Wally and her father. The police officer consented and the two launches churned away. As the others waved good-bye to the police boats, the station wagon pulled up. Freddie and Flossie ran to their mother.

"Nan and Daddy are going to sneak up on the crooks and get the boys back," Flossie bubbled.

"Let's hurry to the lookout," Pamela urged.

Kate opened the car door. "Everyone in, then," she said, and drove through a cut in the solid coral rock. The street ended at a small green park beside the sea.

Kate stopped the car. "Here we are," she

announced, and the children rushed out.

Mrs. Channing gazed out at the sea. "Look here!" she called. "The police boats!"

"And way out there is the *Green Moray!*" Dr. Channing said.

When the launches reached the cruiser, three policemen, including the police commissioner, climbed aboard. Five others remained in the rocking craft. The men on deck called down to Wally, Mr. Bobbsey, and Nan to join them.

"Where's the man called Roger?" one of the officers asked.

"Over there," Nan pointed.

"And that's the other fellow we spoke to," Wally said, nodding toward the man with the captain's hat.

"What do you want?" the *Green Moray's* captain asked gruffly.

"We have orders to search your ship, sir," the commissioner said. "Two boys have been kidnapped."

"Be my guest," the captain replied in mock friendliness. Everyone went from room to room but nothing was found.

"We haven't seen the radio yet," Nan whispered to her father.

"There it is, up ahead," he said and looked around. The area was neat and orderly, its walls covered with a variety of knobs, dials, and radio equipment.

Suddenly Nan heard a little thump. "Daddy, what was that?"

The noise persisted. "Seems to be coming from here," Mr. Bobbsey said, moving to a small closet. Before he could reach it, Nan sprang toward the brass knob and yanked it open.

Onto the floor rolled Bert and Tim, tied hand and foot, their mouths gagged with handkerchiefs!

"Come here, quick!" Mr. Bobbsey shouted to the policemen. "We found them!"

As two officers came rushing in, sounds of splashing could be heard outside the cabin.

"Men overboard!" a voice called out.

While the officers raced outside again, Mr. Bobbsey and Nan untied the captives. Bert rubbed his wrists, and Tim Bishop sucked in deep gasps of air. "I thought we were done for," he murmured.

"What happened?" Nan asked.

"Can't tell you now," her brother replied.

"We haven't got a minute to lose." They ran onto the deck in time to see the policemen in the launch haul the dripping escapees from the water. Among them were the captain and Roger.

But this did not seem to interest Bert and Tim at all. They ran to the far side of the *Green Moray* and glanced into the water.

"Dad! Wally! Look down there!"

Bubbles were rising to the surface.

"Divers!" declared Wally.

"Turner and Sanderson are down there searching for the treasure on the old pirate ship," Tim said. "They've located the spot."

Wally grabbed Mr. Bobbsey's arm. "Do you know how to dive?"

"Yes. I did some in the service."

"Good. Come with me." The two men hopped back into the second launch where Wally flung open a long locker. From it he pulled out two diving outfits.

The police, meanwhile, prodded their prisoners back onto the deck of the *Green Moray*. The dripping men, shackled securely, looked glumly into the water. Great masses of bubbles burped to the surface.

"Oh, there's a fight going on down there!" Nan quavered.

The words had hardly passed her lips when two heads sheathed in black rubber bobbed out of the waves. The divers, minus face masks, were pale and gasping for breath.

"Turner and Sanderson!" Tim shouted.

"Poor fish!" Nan cried gleefully.

The kidnappers were followed by two other black suits, swimming up easily from below. Wally and Mr. Bobbsey guided their captives to the side of the cruiser where strong arms lifted the exhausted pair on deck. They flopped down, glaring angrily at the twins.

"If they hadn't come to Bermuda, we wouldn't be in this mess!" the man with the scarred lip said.

"What do you mean? It was you who thought they would recognize your picture!" Sanderson snapped.

Two of the policemen stood guard over the prisoners while a third man threw a towline to the launches. Then, after Wally made a careful note of their location, the *Green Moray* slithered toward shore.

On the way, Bert and Tim told him about their wild ride in the glass-bottom boat. "We got out of the Turtle's Head cave just in time," Bert began. "There wasn't an inch of headroom to spare as the tide rolled in."

The boys explained that Turner and Sanderson had made a beeline for the *Green*

Moray. Once they were aboard, the thieves sank Wally's boat.

"Just as long as they didn't sink you!" the diver declared.

"How did you send the radio message?" Mr. Bobbsey asked his son.

"I managed to prop myself up just enough to flip on the radio with two fingers. Then I kept whispering into the mike, hoping somebody would hear."

"We did!" said Nan, beaming.

Nan noticed that Tim looked rather sad.

"What's the matter? You seem almost sorry to be rid of your crooked friends," she said.

"No—but I still wish I'd found that treasure!"

Wally grinned broadly. "Well, maybe we can look for it together."

Tim leaped to his feet happily. "Want to dive for treasure?" he asked Bert.

"You bet!"

"Then we'll start tomorrow," Wally promised.

The captured ship arrived alongside the big dock. Among the first to greet the triumphant party were Mrs. Bobbsey,

Freddie and Flossie, the Channings, and Kate. Kate flung herself at Tim and they hugged while tears flowed down their faces.

Mrs. Bobbsey kissed Bert, who grinned in embarrassment. "Thank goodness, you're safe!" she sighed. Little did she know that the Bobbseys would soon be on the trail of another exciting adventure at home, *The Dune Buggy Mystery*.

After the prisoners were led off to the police station, details of the mystery were revealed in the commissioner's office.

Turner and Sanderson who were petty thieves in London had decided to turn treasure hunters.

"But they weren't too good at it," Wally said, shaking his head.

"That's right," the commissioner agreed. "So they tried to steal relics from our museum. The first clues weren't revealed until you Bobbseys came to visit Bermuda."

"You mean old Mr. Simpson's description of the men?" Nan queried.

"Yes. By the way, you were right about Queen Sweets. Turner is crazy about them. We found a big bag of them among his belongings."

The commissioner also explained that Turner never wanted to have his picture taken. "And when you snapped him at the airport, Bert, he was desperate to get the film."

"Then he and Sanderson followed us on the motorcycle," Bert deduced. "And one of them sent the warning note."

"I have a question," Pamela spoke up.

"Yes?" the commissioner asked.

"How did you know these men were thieves in London?"

The officer chuckled. "We sent out fingerprints that were taken from that radio set they left behind at Walter's place. They were identified by the London police as Turner's and Sanderson's. Turner is pretty clever. In London the bobbies call him 'Slippery Sam.' "

At the mention of the name the Bobbseys shrieked.

"You really mean it?" Nan asked.

"Why, yes. What's so strange?"

The young detectives laughed until tears came into their eyes. "We caught Slippery Sam after all!" Freddie exclaimed.